This in**cred-ible** Scholastic book belongs to:

ZOO

SHOP

CLOSED

For Matthew, Wendy, Sami,
Joe, Jenna and Zak – S.L.

First published in 2017 by Scholastic Children's Books

Euston House,

24 Eversholt Street

London

NW1 1DB

A division of Scholastic Ltd

www.scholastic.co.uk

London • New York • Sydney

Auckland • Mexico City

New Delhi

Hong Kong

TIGERS

LIONS

BEARS

OH MY!

Illustrations copyright © 2017 Steven Lenton
Text copyright © 2017 Scholastic Children's Books
Concept and design by Strawberrie Donnelly • Written by Sophie Cashell

PB ISBN 978 1407 16611 7
All rights reserved • Printed in China
1 3 5 7 9 10 8 6 4 2

The moral rights of Steven Lenton have been asserted.
Papers used by Scholastic Children's Books are made from wood grown in sustainable forests.

LET'S FIND FRED

Steven Lenton

Fred's House

SCHOLASTIC

It was early evening at Garden City Zoo and all of the animals were safely snuggled in their beds, ready to sleep. Stanley the zookeeper had just finished singing a lullaby to Ellie and Mellie the elephants and was off to tell Fred a bedtime story.

But Fred wasn't ready for bed.
He had other ideas.

He dreamt of candyfloss,
balloons and parties.

Fred wanted to have . . .

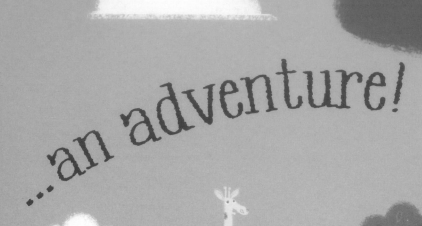

Stanley jumped on his squeaky old scooter and sped after Fred.

ZOO

CITY

PARK

MAZE

CINEMA

PANDA POST

CAB

He zipped and zoomed through the traffic.

"That pesky panda's no match for a clever zookeeper like ME!" he cried.

"Now, if only that bus wasn't blocking my view."

Stanley arrived at the City Market and stared keenly around.

And **there** he was!

"Fred's large, round and fluffy — I'll find him in no time."

Fred was having an **excellent** time.
He'd made new friends,

been to a **concert**,

and tried some ice cream.
(Which was very good, but not
quite as tasty as candyfloss.)

Far away, Fred could hear a familiar voice calling him.
But Fred **still** wasn't ready for bed.

Oh no!

Fred!

Fred!

Fred!

Poor Stanley was NOT having an excellent time. He huffed and puffed his way around the park, searching in every corner. He couldn't see Fred anywhere. Stanley called out loudly,

"Can anyone help me find Fred? He's

ENTRANCE

THE
PAND-A-MAZE

MARKET
MAZE
ZOO
FUNFAIR

"Try the Pand-a-Maze," a friendly
woman suggested. "It's the
perfect place for a bear to hide."

a panda and it's past his bedtime!"

Stanley made his way through the maze.

over him.

DEAD END!

LOOMED

It was dark and the walls

It was a little bit

scary,

even for a brave zookeeper

like Stanley.

There were bear-shaped

shadows everywhere

YOU ARE HERE

but none belonged to Fred.

"Fred, where **are** you?" Stanley cried out.

EXIT →

TOUR GUIDE

He listened hard for a reply,

but all he could hear was

the echo of soft footsteps disappearing

into the distance.

Fred knew he should wait for Stanley, but there was ONE more place he wanted to visit…

The Funfair!

GHOST TRAIN

After trying out every ride at the fair, Fred started to feel a bit dizzy.
He stumbled over to a bench, his arms piled high
with clouds of candyfloss.

He settled
down to eat,

and eat,

and...

"Uh‑‑oh!"

Fred fled as fast as his legs could carry him... through the Art Gallery

with Stanley hot on his heels.

Stanley's chest
heaved up and down
as he raced after Fred.

He slipped
and slid
down the
gallery stairs,
flew

across

the

crossing

other side . . .
on the
building
towering
into the
UP
up,
and

Into the biggest **panda** **party** of them all!

"But where is Fred?"